The Sketchbook

This Book was gi...
Kettering Baptis...

a story by Mojo Place

Purple Ducks Publishing

Purple Ducks Digital Media
Granby, Connecticut

Published by Purple Ducks Publishing
a division of Purple Ducks Digital Media, Inc.
POB 251, Granby, CT 06035
www.purpleducks.com

This is a work of fiction. Names, characters, places and incidents are either
the product of the author's overactive imagination or used
fictitiously. Any resemblance to actual events, locales or persons
(living or dead) is coincidental. So there. Nyaaahh.

ISBN-13: 978-0-9815365-0-7 (hardcover)
ISBN-13: 978-0-9815365-1-4 (trade paperback)
ISBN-13: 978-0-9815365-2-1 (ebook)

Library of Congress Control Number: 2011909717

Purple Ducks
Publishing

For my friend Perry,
who is an awesome artist

Chapter 1

The Painter lived down the road from me, out in the country, in a small house perched on top of a hill.

It was an odd, knicky-knacky sort of house, just the type you'd expect an artist to have. It was full of little nooks and dead ends, as if the builder had no real plans and just slapped the rooms together. Its oddest quirk was that the front of the house—or, at least, the side that looked like a front, with a porch, shutters, hedges and all—did not face the road. It looked in the opposite direction, down the hill, as if it were too busy admiring the view to bother with the other houses on the street.

The Painter was kind of like that, too. She lived in her own little world, and those who didn't bother to introduce themselves were ignored. It wasn't that she didn't like her neighbors. She was a nice enough person once you got to know her. She was just too busy to get out and socialize, and folks tended to leave her alone. Over the years all sorts of rumors spread about her. The grownups thought she was weird, snobbish, and perhaps a little crazy. The children had their own ideas—much more imaginative theories, usually involving witchcraft, a hidden dungeon and some nameless mystery victim who vanished years ago and was never.... seen.... *again*.

While all these rumors whispered their way around the neighborhood, do you know what the Painter was really doing within the crazy walls of that crazy house?

She was painting.

Her neighbors never guessed it (they never asked) but their secretive, mad neighbor was actually a world-famous artist, a celebrity in the big-city world of museums and collectors. I won't bother you with her name, for that would give her away. But you can walk into just about any art museum in the country and see her work displayed. And that strange-looking house held not torture devices nor counterfeit money printers, but hundreds of her paintings, hanging on the walls or leaning carelessly against them.

Yeah, I know, paintings aren't as exciting as gold coins or rare jewels, but trust me: her paintings were worth an awful lot of money. If the art world knew about it, her ramshackle house would be priceless. But no one knew about it—not agents, nor neighbors, nor insurance adjusters, nor art collectors. Nobody knew— and that's how the Painter liked it. She painted not for money or fame anymore, but just for the sheer joy of painting.

The Painter bought this house a few years ago when she retired, mostly because she liked the view. From her front porch (or back porch, depending on how you looked at it) the countryside spread out like a huge living canvas. Fields and forests, houses and barns, with a winding river sewing it all together. A range of small mountains, swelling like furry green bubbles, framed the distant horizon.

There was always something new to see. Early in the morning, the fog settled into the valleys, giving the mountains a floating, ghost-like appearance. During the day, after the fog burned off, the houses and sharp steeples of the village dragged the eye away from the soft greens of the countryside. In the evening, the hard lines softened in the fading light and the mountains moved forward once more, swallowing the town as night closed in. Later, even the mountains vanished against the black sky. The only things visible then were the stars above, and the town lights below reflecting them.

The Painter liked to sit on her porch and watch this scene unfold for hours, until long after the sun disappeared behind the mountains. The beauty of it all struck her deeply. The longer she sat and watched the stronger she felt. Finally one day she decided to capture the scene on canvas. Somehow she knew in her heart it would be her greatest work.

Since this was to be a special painting, she prepared more carefully than usual. The average store-bought canvas would never do. She built her own, ten feet long and five feet tall, in her garage. She put just as much care into building the canvas as she would painting it. The wooden frame had mitered corners cut exactly on the 45th degree. The pieces of wood fit together without an overlap or a crack to be seen. She stretched a piece of canvas over this frame and wrapped it around the back. She held the cloth in place with heavy metal staples, evenly spaced along the entire frame, hidden in back where no one would see them.

The finished product was as tight as a drum. She then primed it, as they call it, with a special white gooey paint. It stiffened the fabric and filled in all the tiny holes in the weave of the cloth, leaving a nice smooth clean surface for the paint.

It was a great deal of work, more than she usually bothered with, but the Painter wanted everything just right. She felt proud of her canvas when she dragged it out of her garage and set it up in her front (or back) yard. It was a beautiful piece of craftsmanship, a work of art in itself. It seemed almost a shame to dirty it with paint.

(Most people fail to see the skill involved in making a canvas. All they see is a blank canvas. And if that canvas remains blank, they begin to feel cheated. Don't worry; before this story is over you'll have your painting. You just have to be patient. Our Painter does not like to be rushed. If we bother her now, she won't paint, and if she doesn't paint, there'll be no story, and if there's no story, then all these words I've already written will be just a big waste of everybody's time.)

The Painter thought her blank canvas was beautiful, but she could also imagine her finished painting upon it. That vision so excited her she could hardly wait to start—yet at the same time it frightened her. The canvas didn't seem so large when she was making it. Now it looked so big and empty she didn't know where to begin.

Her mind felt as if a dozen people were inside, all talking at once. One voice told her to start with the mountains. Another suggested the curving line of the river. Still another advised her to forget the whole thing and take up some easier hobby, like writing. At least writers have a place to start: at the top of the page. The Painter had the added burden of deciding where to put the first mark on this big, beautiful canvas.

To top it all off, she wasn't feeling well. She wasn't exactly sick, just really tired. It was probably due to spending the past couple of days in her stuffy old garage, building the canvas. There were some old paint cans in there, and paint fumes and the car smells must have made her woozy. Whatever the reason, she felt exhausted. Too tired to make any important decisions.

The Painter covered her canvas with a piece of clear plastic to protect it from the weather. She vowed to begin her work the very next morning, after a good night's sleep. Maybe then she would feel better, she thought to herself. Maybe then she would know where to start.

Chapter 2

The Painter was one of those awful types who liked to get up at dawn. While normal people slept, she ate breakfast and walked out to the canvas. She brought with her the tools she would need to paint: three cans of paint, a jar of thinner, and a big brush. She also had a charcoal pencil and a brand-new pad of newsprint, which is a type of cheap, flimsy paper. She used the newsprint to draw out her ideas before she committed them to the canvas. Even though she could paint over any mistakes she made, she didn't want to needlessly mark that beautiful clean surface.

She sat down in the grass and flipped open her new sketchbook. She meant to draw a bit, just to loosen up her arm and to get the feel for what she was painting. The sun coming up behind her, however, filled the scene with such beauty and color she forgot about drawing. If you've ever watched the sun come up you know what I mean. The sun doesn't pop up like a toaster. It comes up as slowly as a flower blooms. You can sit and stare for hours and nothing seems to be happening. Then all of a sudden you realize that something *has* happened, and what was once wrapped in darkness is now blooming and alive with color. It sneaks up on you, and time stands still.

The Painter didn't know how long she sat there before she roused herself and looked down at her opened sketchbook. It seemed silly to draw out the scene on paper first. She saw it every day. She knew it by heart. Besides, it was spread out perfectly in front of her, just waiting to be appreciated.

But the blank paper beckoned and the charcoal pencil dangled from her fingers. Its newly sharpened point begged to be used. She looked at the pencil, at the canvas, and at the paper. Then she drew a small charcoal circle on the newsprint, just to loosen up her arm and get her in the mood to draw.

The act of dirtying the paper relieved some of the tension she felt about marking up the canvas. With this relief came a bit of silliness. The circle reminded her of one of those smiley faces, she decided. She added two dots for eyes and giggled. She was about to add a big, curving smile, but she grew suddenly embarrassed. A great artist like herself—about to begin the most important painting of her career—and here she was drawing smiley faces in her sketchbook! She felt foolish, and she looked around to see if anyone was watching. She dropped the pad on the grass and turned her attention to the empty canvas, adjusting her mood to a more serious, more productive, more *artistic* frame of mind. Smiley faces, indeed!

She looked from the blank canvas to the scene before her, seeing not hills and mountains and houses but a pattern of curves and lines: the gentle slopes of the fields, the steeper curves of the mountains beyond. The evergreen forest was a curved wedge, forcing itself between two fields, and here and there a barn or a church popped up like a wart on the line of the landscape.

She chose one of these lines, guessed its proportions on canvas and moved her charcoal pencil along that imaginary line—once, twice, thrice—without making a mark. Then she made the movement a fourth time, and, almost accidentally, the black point touched the canvas and dragged along its surface, bumping over the interwoven threads, leaving a sharp black wake on the fabric.

Once the first line committed itself, everything else fell into place. She began to add other lines, glancing up repeatedly at the real life display. These marks were the skeleton, the framework of her creation. She would build upon it, layer after layer of different colored paints. Somehow, somewhere in the process, it would come alive. She knew she could never get her painting as perfect as it appeared—she could never match the trees leaf for leaf or the grass blade for blade—but she could capture the essence, the feelings the scene produced.

As the Painter sketched, she found her eyes drawn to the crude face on the paper at her feet. Was it her imagination, or were those two pencil-dot eyes watching her? She told herself she was crazy and went back to work. Before long she found herself looking down at the paper again.

It bothered her. It bothered her *a lot*. She liked to work alone. An observer, even an imaginary one, was intolerable.

Then she laughed at herself. Here was she, a great painter, letting her imagination run away with her! She was glad nobody was there to see this. She ripped the sheet of paper off the pad, ready to crumple it into a ball and throw it aside. But the eyes seemed to plead with her. She found herself making excuses. It was a perfectly good piece of paper, hardly used at all. She could not bring herself to waste it. So instead she drew two circles around the pencil-dot eyes, like eyelids. She made sure the eye-dots were fixed at the bottom, so the face was looking down at the ground instead of up at her. She then tossed the paper to one side. With one last suspicious glare at those downcast eyes, she went back to her sketching.

It was absorbing work, filling all that canvas. She concentrated so hard on it nothing else in the world mattered. She did make a couple of mistakes, a line or two slightly misjudged, but each time she pulled a kneaded eraser out of her pocket and scrubbed it out. A faint shadow remained, scarcely noticeable. It would soon be covered by paint.

(A kneaded eraser works just like a regular rubber eraser. It even looks a little like one, fresh out of the package, but it is softer and squishier and you can mold it like a piece of clay. You can stretch it apart and mash it together and fold it and twist it and have a grand old time. They're loads of fun to play with, even if you don't erase anything.)

When the Painter finally stood back to take a rest, she realized just how late it was getting. The sun was blazing overhead. It must be close to lunchtime. Working out in the open with the sun bouncing off the canvas made her eyes ache. She didn't notice anything while she was working, but once she stepped away she realized she was exhausted.

Still, it was good work. She stepped back to look at the whole canvas—and her eyes fell once more on the piece of paper on the ground, a splash of white against the dark green grass.

The face's eyes were looking *up*.

Chapter 3

The Painter's stomach went funny, as if she had just swallowed a chunk of ice. She watched the eyes sweep over her canvas, scanning it from top to bottom. When a breeze ruffled the paper, it even looked like the head was trying to crane around to see more.

Then the eyes turned to the Painter. For a moment they regarded her, curious, but when it saw her shocked, open-mouthed expression a look of guilt flashed across the face. The eyes moved quickly back down to the ground, pretending nothing had happened.

Not daring to believe her own sun-bleared eyes, the Painter picked up the piece of paper and studied it closely. She could see the graininess of the charcoal on the smooth surface. She saw the eyes fixed to the bottom of the paper, as lifeless as a statue. She could—

There! Did you see it? For just a second—the eyes looked up again! It was only a flicker of movement, but it happened!

Determined now, the Painter set to work with her pencil. She drew a big smile that took up most of the lower portion of the face. Then, feeling rather foolish, she held the paper up to her face and spoke to it.

"Hello!" she called, shaking the paper to get the face's attention. "Can you talk? Who are you?"

The eyes looked at her dumbly. The Painter pointed at her own lips and exaggerated their movement as she spoke.

"I said, can you talk?"

The face seemed surprised it had a mouth. It opened and closed it a couple of times, and smiled. The Painter smiled back.

"Can you speak?" she asked. "Say something!"

The eyes narrowed, the mouth frowned. Then, the face spoke—a faint, scratchy sound, like a pencil point on paper—but a distinct voice forming distinct words.

"What's that?" the face said. "I can't hear you!"

The Painter felt a rush of emotions: Disbelief, relief, amusement. Disbelief because she was actually talking to one of her drawings. Relief because the drawing was talking back, proving (she hoped) that she wasn't really going crazy. And amusement because she never once thought to draw the face ears. She could have yelled all day and the face couldn't hear her.

She quickly drew on two ears, two small ovals, one on each side. One turned out a little bigger than the other, giving the face a lopsided appearance. With its king-sized mouth and its new ears, the sketch looked more childish than ever. But the Painter felt oddly pleased with her new creation.

"How's that?" she asked, sitting back from her work.

The face smiled. "Much better." Its eyes darted around. "This is a beautiful place," it added. "Did you do all this yourself?"

The Painter looked around her—at the canvas, at the green fields, at the trees and the houses and the mountains.

"No, of course not," she laughed. "The canvas is mine. Everything else was already here. I'm just copying it today."

"It's all very pretty," the face said. "Could I see it again, please? The white thing you've been marking, I mean."

The face's blank side was facing the canvas. The Painter obligingly turned it around. She held the face up close so it could see the detail work, then far away so it could see the whole picture. The face responded with appreciative "oooohs" and "aaaahhhhs".

The Painter warmed under its flattery and stopped feeling so self-conscious about talking to a piece of paper. Somewhere in that charcoal circle there was a bright, enthusiastic brain that knew good work when it saw it. True, its features could only function on two dimensions, but since when could a body imprison a mind?

"Gosh, this is great!" The face looked at the Painter with unabashed reverence. "What do you call this stuff, anyway?"

"Huh?" It never occurred to her that someone might not know what she was doing. "It's a painting. I'm a painter, you see."

"Painting!" the face repeated.

"Well, not exactly, yet," the Painter admitted. "Right now, it's just a charcoal sketch, like yourself. But when I'm done drawing, I'll lay the paint on top of it. *Then* I'll have a painting."

All this was illustrated with hand gestures, pantomiming sketching and brushstrokes. But it was all beyond the scope of the charcoal face.

"What's paint?" it asked.

"Paint?"

Such utter basics of life! How would you explain food to someone who never needs to eat? Such was the Painter's dilemma. Paint, to her, was such a simple, necessary concept—so simple, she could not find the proper words to describe it.

"Paint?" she stammered. "It's pigment. You know. Color. Mixed up with some sort of liquid so it sticks to the canvas." She stopped, realizing her answer was hardly enlightening. The face listened politely, but nothing registered in those charcoal-dot eyes. She gave up with a shrug. "You'll understand what I'm talking about when I start painting."

"Do you think you could teach *me* how to do that?" the face asked. "It sounds really neat!"

A twinge of misgiving shot through the Painter, as it always did when someone asked her to teach them.

"That would be impossible," she laughed.

"Impossible?" If ever there was a disappointed face, it was this one. Its mouth turned down, its eyes widened, and although they were only paper and charcoal they seemed to glisten with tears. "But why? I've watched you. It doesn't look that hard to me."

"Yes, but I am equipped to draw," the Painter replied. "I have hands and feet. I have the strength to pick up a pencil or a brush. You're just a sketch on a piece of paper. You couldn't possibly do anything."

"Just a sketch," the face murmured, with downcast eyes. It was silent for a while, depressed as it realized just how limited a face on paper could be. Then an idea struck it and the eyes flew up once more, wide and wild with hope.

"You could draw me hands!" it pleaded. "You could draw me hands and feet and you could draw me a pencil to use! Oh, please give me a body! Please, please, please!"

The Painter felt slightly put out. Next time, she thought, I must remember not to make the mouth so big. But she recognized ingenuity when she saw it.

Anyone who could find a way around such staggering limitations deserved all the help they could get.

Still, it was an annoying imposition. What more would the face require? Its own studio? Its own house in the country? Would she be spending all her time drawing tiny amenities of life, just so a stupid smiley face would keep smiling?

She was too enthralled with her new creation to deny it anything, though. She drew the face a body: a stick torso, and stick arms and legs with stick fingers and toes.

The charcoal sketch watched the whole time, observing every detail as he changed from a simple face into a crude stickman. Not knowing any better, he thought his body quite beautiful, and he couldn't wait to try it out. He flexed his arms as the Painter drew his legs, and wiggled his toes the instant they were finished.

"Stop squirming," the Painter admonished at one point. "You'll come out all shaky."

When his whole body was completed, the stickman tried a few jumping jacks and walked from one edge of the paper to the other. It was odd to watch, for he could only move in the two dimensions of the paper and his markings seemed to glide over the paper's surface.

The stickman was pleased. The Painter watched him walk around, getting used to his new body. When he seemed to have gained good control, she drew a short line near him on the page.

"Okay, Sketch," she said, unconsciously naming him

as she spoke. "There's your pencil. Start drawing."

Sketch stooped to pick it up, but he could not lift the pencil point off the page. A line was drawn the instant he moved it. He was delighted anyway, and set to work scribbling all over his paper. The Painter watched him indulgently for a while, but her own work beckoned. It would be too late to paint today, but she still had some last minute details she wished to add with the charcoal.

For the first time her beloved masterpiece-to-be paled next to that sheet of newsprint lying on the grass. Her canvas didn't interest her as much anymore. A newer thrill of discovery had touched her—the thrill of a miracle. A simple, ordinary stickman—something a child could draw—held her strangely fascinated.

She watched as Sketch scribbled all over his paper, oblivious to anything else. Was he alive? Was he for real? How could she test her sanity? Walk up to some stranger, thrust a piece of paper in his face and ask, "Is this drawing talking to you? Can you see it move?"

She didn't even want to think about it. People thought she was crazy enough as it was, without doing *that*.

Sighing, she turned back to her canvas, admiring the work she had already done. It felt good to her, and her instincts had never failed her before. She stepped back and surveyed the view as she had every day for years. She lingered on long-memorized details—visiting old friends, really—seeing more with her heart than with her eyes. The thrill was still there, a deep catch in her

breath that refused to be exhaled; every good human
emotion condensed into one tiny pocket deep within. It
felt right. So long as that feeling remained, she figured,
she couldn't be wrong. She couldn't be insane.

Her confidence thus renewed, she resumed sketching
with purpose, and soon lost herself again in the joy of
creation. Everything else in the world—even walking,
talking stickmen—melted into an impressionistic
background. Soft pastels and blurred outlines mean
little to those who do not look closer. The Painter made
a similar decision not to think about things anymore.
Nothing in the world mattered to her except her canvas.

She was almost finished when Sketch interrupted, his
thin voice shrieking over the afternoon breeze.

"Painter! Oh, Painter! Look!"

The Painter turned to Sketch. Most of the paper was
covered with meaningless scrawls. The stickman himself
was standing in the last blank corner.

"Very nice, Sketch," she said. She didn't mean it, of
course, but she said it just to be nice. Underneath all the
grumbling she was a good-hearted person. She didn't
want to hurt anyone's feelings, not even a stickman's.

"No, look!" Sketch insisted. His attention was focused
not on the scribbles around him, but on the corner of the
paper, near his left foot. The paper was curling out and
in, out and in, regular as a pendulum.

"See that?" he exclaimed. *"I'm* doing that!"

At first, the Painter thought it was the breeze tugging
on the paper. But no, it *was* the stickman! The Painter

could see slight changes in the lines she had drawn for Sketch's legs. They thickened and shortened as the paper pulled out and relaxed again as the paper drew back. Sketch's eyes, as they moved from his leg to the Painter's face, were alight with excitement.

"I could walk like you can!" he blurted. "I could control the paper, if it were only smaller. Can you take away some of the paper?"

The Painter was growing fond of her resourceful little Sketch. It saddened her to have to correct him.

"It's not as easy as it looks," she said gently. "If I were to cut you out, you could probably move the paper. Problem is, the paper is only newsprint. It has no strength. I have bones inside of me. You do not. You would flop around like a rag doll. The slightest wind would knock you off your feet."

Sketch looked so upset at this the Painter felt badly. His whole face fell, and wells of charcoal tears appeared on his lower eyelids. One drop broke through and dribbled down his cheek, leaving a thin black line.

"Oh, come now, don't cry!" the Painter exclaimed, sitting in the grass and picking up the paper. She tried to rub the tear marks away with her pinkie, but the charcoal smudged. Reaching for her kneaded eraser, she twisted an end into a fine point and carefully rubbed the line away. "It's not as bad as all that. Really, I think you would be safer on the paper, anyway. Much safer. You'd be less likely to be ripped, and—"

A grasshopper jumped onto the paper, distracting

her. She shooed it off and it made a flying leap over to the canvas. It sat where it landed for a few seconds, then crawled to the top and jumped off into the grass.

The Painter thought hard. Less likely to be ripped. Yes, it just might work! Her tone changed from apology to enthusiasm.

"You know something?" she asked excitedly. "There's a whole bunch of animals out there that do not have bones, but they get around just as well as people do. Sometimes even better."

"How?" Sketch sniffled.

"They have a coat of armor around their bodies, like a skin, only much harder. It supports them and protects them."

"What's armor?"

"Never mind. Scientists call it an exoskeleton, which means, well, having your bones on the outside. Grasshoppers and other bugs have them. That's why they crunch when you step on them."

Sketch shuddered, but the Painter was too excited to notice.

"Look, I could give you an exoskeleton, of sorts," she said. "I could paste you onto cardboard and cut you out. I could bend the cardboard in the right places to make joints, so you could move your arms and legs. Then perhaps you could walk around as well as anyone."

The Painter struggled to her feet and hurriedly cleaned up for the day. She pocketed the pencil, placed the paint cans, the brush and the jar of thinner close to the canvas, and covered everything with the plastic sheet. She then picked up the paper and the sketchbook and ran to the house. The newsprint stickman fluttered in the wind the whole way.

Chapter 4

Sketch endured the wild ride as best as he could. He couldn't have fallen off the paper if he wanted to, but the constant flapping in the wind made him feel ill. He was glad when the Painter threw him down on the kitchen table.

The Painter rummaged through her cupboards and drawers, looking for materials to work with. She found some glue and a stencil-cutter, a triangular blade set in a metal handle. It was as sharp as a scalpel. But the only cardboard she could find was a heavy corrugated box, which was too thick to use. She dashed upstairs and came down with a nice thin shirt-box she was saving for wrapping presents. She used the heavier cardboard to work on, to protect her tabletop from harm.

It was most exciting and interesting for Sketch. First he was placed face down on the work area. A cold bead of glue smeared along his back. Then the Painter gingerly picked him up by the corners and pressed the paper against the thin cardboard. She rubbed gently, being careful not to smudge the charcoal, until the paper was glued firmly. Finally, with the stencil-cutter, the Painter cut him out, leaving a thin white border of paper all around him for extra support.

Even with the border, it was a ticklish process. The Painter was very slow, gentle and cautious. Sketch did his best not to flinch, but seeing that steel blade cut so close to him made him very nervous. Soon it was over, and the Painter bent the cardboard in all the right places: at the neck, waist, elbows, wrists, knees and ankles. When she was finished, she placed Sketch upright on the table, letting him stand on his own flap-like feet for the first time. She stepped back, beaming.

"How does it feel?" she asked.

Sketch could only stand stiffly and smile back, too afraid to move. He wavered, but kept his balance.

"Oh, it's great!" he murmured. "I never dreamed—"

He broke off to concentrate on his feet. Slowly, one foot shuffled out a tiny fraction, and the other moved out to meet it.

"Put all your weight on one foot as you move the

other out," the Painter instructed, for she realized Sketch knew nothing about three-dimensional walking.

Sketch leaned to one side, lifted a foot off the tabletop, and, paper arms flailing wildly, tumbled flat. He propped himself up, bent his knees, and scrambled to his feet. He fell again...and again...and...then...he was standing once more.

"This will take some practice!" he said.

"Are you hurt?" the Painter asked anxiously.

"Hurt? What does that mean?" Sketch replied.

The Painter then remembered that Sketch wasn't flesh and blood, but a charcoal drawing. It was so easy, when she talked to him, to forget he wasn't a real person.

Sketch was all set to enjoy his new freedom.

"After I learn to walk properly, will you teach me to paint?" he asked.

The Painter shrugged uncomfortably.

"I don't know, Sketch," she said. "I'm not very good with students."

"Why not?" Sketch looked up from his feet and frowned. "Is painting that difficult?"

"No, it's not that," she sighed, suddenly feeling miserable. "I used to teach quite a bit, back when I needed the money. But—I don't know. I just don't get along with people, I guess."

"Why not?" Sketch smiled shyly. "You seem like a nice person to me."

"Well, yeah, I like to think I am," she agreed. "I just don't like how people are taught to think. Or, rather, taught *not* to think. It drives me nuts. People don't want to think for themselves anymore. They just want the answers handed to them, like burgers at a drive-through. That's not learning. That's memorizing. Can you see the difference?"

"No."

"Well, don't feel bad. Neither can anybody else." She sighed, feeling her blood pressure rise just thinking about it. "A lot of things can be taught because they're cut and dried facts," she said. "Things like multiplication tables and state capitals. Two times two is four. The capital of New York is Albany. Facts. You get it?"

"Uh, huh," Sketch said, but a bit too politely; more to appease her than anything. The Painter swallowed her annoyance as best as she could.

"Well, there's very little facts in art. You can teach the basics, like technique—brushstrokes, or how to mix colors, or how to wedge clay, or how to read music. You can even teach them some general rules about composition and line and color."

"Can you teach me the rules?" Sketch asked.

"Really good things don't always go by a rule book," the Painter snapped. "You have to get past that type of thinking. You have to jump into this abyss of uncertainty. It's filled with all sorts of beautiful, elusive, terrifying things. Most people don't want to jump. They stay on the cliff and make others do the jumping for them and ask them what it's like. No matter how hard you try, you can't convince them that they have to jump themselves if they're ever going to understand any of it."

"Do they get hurt?" Sketch asked.

"It's a figure of speech, okay? They don't really jump. Look, you can say that a painting is a fact, right? It exists. It's a solid, material thing. It can be measured. It is made up of this much canvas and that much wood, and so much red paint, blue paint, white paint, and so on. There are people who think that way. And there's nothing wrong with this. It's a very helpful, useful way to look at the world."

"Facts!" Sketch said, proudly.

"Right!" the Painter nodded. "But if a painting just used facts, then anyone could make a painting. It would be like following a recipe. Take three cups of blue paint, add one half-cup of red, and glop it on the canvas."

"Facts!" Sketch repeated.

"But it doesn't work that way!" the Painter said, growing louder in her mounting frustration. "Even the greatest fact-finders in the world can't figure out creation. They dissect living things down to their cells, down to structures within those cells, down to molecules and atoms and even beyond that. Yet they still don't know how the thing they're ripping apart became alive in the first place!"

"Do you?" Sketch asked, trying to be helpful.

The Painter expelled her breath in an irritated noise, flinging her arms up to clasp her head. Sketch visibly drooped, afraid that her passion and fury was somehow his fault.

"No," she said, with a forced, measured calm. "There's a thing in physics they call relativity. In the art world, we call it perspective. An object changes depending on how you look at it. There's no one perspective. Things shift around, depending on what angle you look at them—high, low, near, far, upside down, rightside up. What's more, *how* you observe affects *what* you observe. If you try to find life by cutting open some poor animal, you will destroy that life in the process."

"Will looking at a painting destroy the painting?" Sketch asked.

"Yeah, sometimes," the Painter laughed. "I've analyzed several paintings to death, trying to figure out why I like them. I've tried and tried, but I can't explain *why* it's alive. I just *know* it is."

"Could you teach me these things?" Sketch asked, timidly.

"WHO KNOWS?" the Painter shouted. "That's why I don't teach people anymore! They all want to be *taught* something...but none of them wants to *learn*!"

Sketch trembled under her wrath. He had never experienced anything like this in his short life, and he didn't know what to make of it. The Painter's violent harangue left him confused and frightened. It was as if she was speaking a foreign language. He wanted to say something that would ease her anger.

"Why don't you tell them what you told me?" he asked.

The Painter pulled her kneaded eraser out of her pocket and ripped it viciously in half, then mashed the two spongy halves back together and stretched it in half again.

"I've tried," she said quietly. "But people don't listen. Art isn't one of the great mysteries of life anymore. It's something used to decorate the walls. And heaven help you if it doesn't match the couch." She squeezed the eraser in one hand and smiled wanly, lost in thought.

"*You* aren't going to be much help, either," she added, nodding at Sketch. "How am I going to explain you? You're going to destroy what little credibility I have left."

Sketch wasn't listening. He was staring at the eraser in the Painter's hand, his eyes wide with terror.

"Sketch! What's wrong?"

Sketch trembled violently and gulped once or twice before he could talk.

"I was watching you draw out there on your canvas," he said, his voice quavering. "There was a line—I guess you didn't like it. So you...you—" He closed his eyes for a minute and gulped again. "You took that piece of gray stuff out of your pocket and you rubbed it out. The line wasn't there anymore." He suddenly burst with emotion. "Please don't rub me out! Whatever I did, I promise I won't do it again! Please!"

The Painter looked down at her eraser. She had a

habit of playing with it whenever she was bored or anxious or just thinking about what she would do next. She didn't even realize she had it out now, squeezing and folding it in one hand as she talked.

Her mind felt like it was about to explode. This little drawing was only a few hours old, yet already he had his first lessons in life and death. The Painter recalled scrubbing at the canvas with the eraser, removing that line. She remembered brushing away the little dark crumbs from the bright surface with her pinkie. She never once thought of how the line might feel.

Sketch eyed the eraser nervously and the Painter put it back in her pocket.

"Oh, no!" she exclaimed, her temper forgotten. She placed a reassuring hand on Sketch's back. "I would never do anything like that to you! Sketch, you have to believe me. You mustn't pay any attention to my ranting and raving. I'm just a crazy old woman, that's all. I don't mean anything by it. I would never hurt you. You're my greatest creation, ever. Better than any painting I've ever done. I would sooner draw a mustache on the Mona Lisa than erase you."

Sketch sniffled a bit, uncertain, but he accepted her reassurance with childlike simplicity. A shy smile crept over his face. He hesitated for a few seconds, but his inquisitive nature soon got the better of him.

"What's the Moaning Lisa?" he asked, timidly.

The Painter could see this was going to be a long night.

Chapter 5

Sketch, not needing any sleep, practiced walking all night. By morning he could do many things. Not only could he sit, stand, lie down and get back up, but he could also pick up small articles, like the charcoal pencil the Painter had left on the table. When the Painter came down for breakfast, she found the pencil tip worn down to nothing and her whole table covered with black scribbles.

The Painter grumbled a bit as she cleaned up the mess with paper towels and some liquid cleanser. The wet towels squeaked against the smooth wood as she scrubbed out the marks. This upset Sketch to no end. He wanted to show that her lecture the night before had made an impression. He wanted to prove his willingness to learn. After all, didn't the Painter want Sketch to take after herself and become another great artist?

Wearily the Painter explained—over a hurried breakfast of coffee and buttered toast—what she had already explained several times last night: artists need the proper materials. Her kitchen table, Sketch learned, was not meant to be a canvas.

Sketch proved sensitive to criticism, so the Painter dropped the subject and promised to take him along when she went out to work. Sketch, still testing his new body, wanted to do more than just watch. He wanted to *do* something. So the Painter agreed to bring the pencil and pad of paper along to amuse him.

The Painter felt grumpier than usual that morning. The events of the day before had left her restless all night long. The shock of Sketch coming to life and the constant questions about things she rarely thought about ("Why do you have to go to sleep? Where is sleep?") was wearing on her nerves. She still tried to be nice to Sketch. But the novelty had worn off, leaving only the tiresome weight of responsibility.

They had another argument, right before they left the house. Sketch wanted to show off his newfound skill by walking to the canvas all by himself. The canvas was only a few yards away from the door. It was a short distance by human standards, but for Sketch? Forget it.

The Painter complained that it would take him way too long. Besides, the grass was wet with dew. Water would ruin him. That threat hit home and Sketch agreed to be carried. He insisted on carrying the pencil, though, tightly clenched between his flap-like hands. To his credit, he only dropped it seventeen times.

The Painter took off the plastic that covered the canvas, set it on the grass and placed Sketch on it with the pad of paper. Sketch scribbled away at the top sheet. Before long he grew more interested in what the Painter was doing than his own work. He looked at the huge canvas looming before him, admiring all of the marvelous drawings it contained. None of the lines on the canvas were alive in the sense that Sketch was alive—nothing was moving, anyway. But they seemed alive to him. The stickman could almost see the charcoal trees and grass waving in the breeze.

Sketch remembered bits and pieces of the lecture from the night before. He remembered the Painter said that real art "lived and moved and breathed". Sketch decided that he, himself, must be the best piece of art ever. He was only a stickman, true; but he could go through the motions of living while the more elaborate figures on the canvas remained frozen. Perhaps some people would consider such a though humbling, but not Sketch. He swelled with pride, secure in the Painter's love for her "greatest creation".

Ah, the Painter! What a wonderful, glorious woman she was, Sketch thought. So patient, so loving, so wise. She knew the answer to every question, and she watched over Sketch continually. Squatting on the plastic sheet, his pencil forgotten beside him, Sketch cast loving eyes on his creator and protector, and was immediately mesmerized.

The Painter was messing with a funny round flat-topped thing. Earlier she had called it "blue paint" in her offhand way. Sketch, not wanting to provoke another lecture, didn't ask any further questions, but he didn't understand what the Painter had meant. He watched now with great interest.

With the tapered end of a large brush, the Painter pried the top off the round thing. Then, holding the brush by that same pointy end, she dipped the other end —soft and bristly looking—into the can. She twirled it around, just like she had stirred her coffee that morning at breakfast.

But unlike her coffee spoon, the brush turned colors! The bristles, plain and dark going in, came out of the can a glistening, dazzling deep blue! Sketch had never seen anything like it.

The Painter was not paying any attention to the stickman. She scraped some excess paint off the brush and gazed lovingly at her canvas. Her drawing would soon be hidden under the paint. What was once just black and white would soon burst with color. She hesitated for an instant, but then raised her arm and gave the sky of her painting a big, sweeping smear of blue.

"Blue" is not an adequate name for the color the Painter used. It was a mixture of her own design; she never bothered to name it. Straight out of the can, it seemed almost black, a really deep navy blue. Around the middle of her stroke, where it began to thin, the white of the canvas underneath turned it into a beautiful aquamarine. Further on it thinned out even more into a pastel sky-blue. From there, it was hard to tell where the blue ended and the white canvas resumed.

Once her brush touched the canvas and that marvelous "blue" was applied, Sketch forgot all thoughts of pencil and paper. Why settle for black and white where there is color like that in the world? His yearnings to be an artist grew stronger, until they became a dull ache in his heart.

Now, with long, sweeping strokes, the Painter washed in her sky, using the color she had laid on with her first stroke. She thinned it with a jar of clear liquid and highlighted it here and there with dabs of white paint. In the foreground, it was a nice friendly sky, white fluffy clouds sailing in a pastel-blue sea. Toward the back it blackened with fury, a storm approaching over the mountains. It was beautiful.

"How did you do that?" Sketch blurted, crawling off the plastic and pushing his way through the grass. Luckily for him the sun had dried the dew.

The Painter, mesmerized herself, took a while to break her concentration and answer.

"Hmm? What? Oh—" She smiled, stepped back and

indicated the sky to the west. "Couldn't have asked for a better sky today."

Sketch looked over to where she was pointing. It was a beautiful clear day, but far off, past the mountains, the sky grew dark, just like in her painting. The black, angry-looking clouds scared Sketch for some reason, but he didn't know why. He ignored what he did not understand and turned back to the canvas.

"Could I do that?" he asked.

The Painter was touching up the sky in places, more to be fussy than because it really needed it.

"Well, I suppose you could, if you had enough practice," she said. "I've always been lucky. Painting comes easy to me. But even so I still have to work at it all the time."

"Work?" Sketch could not believe that. The Painter had done it so freely, so easily! Surely it couldn't be work!

"Yes, of course. It's very hard work," the Painter laughed. "What have I been telling you? Painting is more than just slapping paint on a canvas. There's style and technique, the way you use your brush and your paint. It takes a great deal of time and thought and practice to get it just the way you want. Sometimes it never does."

"I thought you just copied what you saw."

"Well, yes and no. If you tried to make an exact copy, you'd go insane. And even if you succeeded, you'd bore people to death. People who look at a still life don't want to see a bowl of fruit. They want to see what the painting says to them with that bowl of fruit."

"What's a still life?"

The Painter sighed. How could she get past these irritating little questions, and back onto the real subject? She took a deep breath and tried again.

"A still life is just one of many subjects you can paint," she said. "Right now, that doesn't matter. Remember, it's *how* you paint that counts, not *what* you paint. Most people try to copy exactly what they see. It's a good exercise for a beginner. Problem is, most people don't see properly. They set a bowl of apples in front of a curtain, and all they see: a bowl of apples. They're so busy trying to get those apples exactly right they don't bother looking for anything else."

"What are apples?" Sketch asked.

"A good painting makes you look twice," the Painter continued loudly, trying to ignore him. "The first glance tells you the facts, what it is—a bowl of apples, a landscape, a person, a scribble. The second glance tells you what the painting has to say to you. Maybe it's the colors the painter used, or the look on the subject's face, or the way the apples are arranged—something speaks to you. That's what I mean when I say the painting lives. It communicates. It talks. It shares its feelings with you."

"So paintings can feel?" Sketch asked. "You mean, just like people?"

"Well, not just paintings," the Painter corrected. "Just about anything will talk to you. It depends on the individual. Paintings don't speak to everyone. Maybe calculus speaks to you, or physics. Maybe quilts, or writing, or housework. It doesn't matter. Art is anything that speaks to you and brings you joy. And don't let any of those snobs using a bunch of really big words tell you otherwise."

"I know how to speak," Sketch said, proudly. "I guess that makes *me* a work of art, huh? I can speak to anyone."

The Painter didn't answer at once. She cleared her throat and glanced over at the painting as if she didn't know what to say.

"I can't really answer that, Sketch," she admitted. "I think you are, sure. But others might not."

"Why not?"

"Before I moved here," the Painter said, "I lived in the city. Before I became famous I made money painting portraits of people. I was good at it. I always tried to look inside the person, instead of just painting brown hair or blue eyes. Whatever qualities that person had—if they were cruel or proud or scared or mean or pleasant—it showed up on the canvas."

"So what?" Sketch wished the Painter would just answer his questions directly, instead of this horrible roundabout way of hers. It only confused him.

"My subjects always reacted differently to the finished product," the Painter said. "Some people liked what they saw, so they liked my paintings. Others didn't like what they saw, so they blamed it on me and called me a bad painter. But scariest of all were those who saw nothing, good or bad. All they ever cared about was whether or not I got their nose right."

"Did you?"

"That doesn't matter," the Painter sighed. "What I'm trying to say is, people are going to have different opinions of you, and nothing you say or do will ever convince them otherwise. Some people will see you as sweet and childlike and friendly, and they'll think you're a work of art because of that. Others will think you're an irritating, juvenile brat. Some will say I'm a crazy old woman, and you're a figment of my imagination. Then there will be those who can't get past the fact that you're a stickman. Forget that you might feel and talk and move around. Forget even that you might be the best-drawn stickman in the whole world. They won't see a work of art. All they'll ever see is a stickman."

"Is being a stickman a bad thing?" Sketch asked.

"Well, it's not *bad*," the Painter said. "It's just too ordinary for some people. People think they want exciting, different things. They'll say there's nothing special about *you*. You're a stickman. *Anyone* can draw a stickman."

"Is that true?"

"Well, yeah," the Painter shrugged awkwardly. "But we're all like that. We're all average. Even those who do crazy things to show you how unique they are are just bunched up with all the other terminally unique out there. We're all stickmen, when you get right down to it. That's why you have to look past the obvious. You have to look beyond everything you already know about stickmen if you want to see what makes that one stickman special. Many people aren't going to do that."

The Painter felt suddenly uncomfortable. "Can you see things in your head?" she asked. "I mean, if you close your eyes, can you still see things?"

"Of course."

"Well, things in your head aren't real. They're called dreams, or visions. Some of them are memories from the past; others are ideas for the future. Some are good, some are bad. They say you should pick one, focus on one good dream, and fix every detail in your mind. If you hold fast to that vision while working hard and perfecting you skills on the outside, some day you will be able to transfer your vision directly to your art. This vision is what gives it life."

"Like your painting," Sketch mused.

"It doesn't have to be a painting. It can be a sculpture, a story, a career, anything once you decide what you want to do. But you have to work hard at it, to prove yourself worthy of it. Truly good things are never just handed to you."

The Painter's words filled Sketch with a marvelous feeling of ambition. He wanted to paint so badly!

"Oh, let me try!" he pleaded, hopping up and down. His arms strained above his head for the brush.

"Haven't you heard anything I've been saying?" the Painter snorted. "You can't start painting right away.

When I fixed it for you to stand by yourself, could you walk all at once? No, of course not. You had to learn. That's how it is with painting, too—or with anything in this world. You have to start at the beginning."

She carried Sketch back over to the plastic and plunked him down next to the pad of paper.

"Here you are," she said, handing him the charcoal pencil. "Start first by learning how to draw. If you need help, just ask, and I'll help you. But I can't teach you anything unless you really want to learn. Get it?"

"Yes, Ma'am," Sketch said. "But when can I learn how to paint? I want to *paint*. You know—like *you*."

"You can start working with color after you've mastered black and white," the Painter said. "Contrast. Light and shadow. The basics. When you've learned how to handle a pencil, I'll give you a paint brush. But not until then."

She didn't need to say any more. Sketch had already flipped the pad to a fresh sheet.

Chapter 6

Sketch attacked the paper with new determination, but despite all his good intentions his scribbles remained just that: scribbles. He didn't realize this. He was proud of his work and he called the Painter over to inspect. He was sure he did a great thing, and deserved to advance to painting right away.

The Painter, though annoyed to be taken away from her work to look at scribbles, was kind. She found some good things to say about his drawings. Her praise led to what she hoped was constructive criticism. Her words were wasted. Sketch wasn't paying attention to what she was saying; he had other thoughts on his mind.

"Painter," he pleaded, "Could you at least make my drawings come to life, like you did with me?"

The Painter was in a spot. She had no control over the stickman coming to life. It just *happened*. None of her other works ever came to life. Nothing on her canvas was wandering around. Sketch was a fluke.

She couldn't admit this in front of him. The little paper and cardboard figure worshipped her. To tell him the truth might tear apart his ultra-sensitive paper soul. Who wants to hear they're an accident? A freak? That, by all laws of nature, they should have never been born?

"Well, ahh, it's not as easy as all that," the Painter said. "I can't bring just any old scribble to life. No—" Here she grasped at another chance to drive her lecture home—"For a drawing to come to life, you can't just scribble aimlessly. You need to start with a vision and believe in that vision while you draw."

Sketch looked at his work with a new eye, a more critical eye.

"But Painter," he said, "I don't have much practice in thinking up visions. Could you give me one, just to start me off?"

"Okay, watch." The Painter picked up the charcoal pencil and ripped down to a fresh piece of paper. "I'm going to draw *you*. You can copy that until you get it right."

Later, when she told me this story, the Painter decided it must had been that particular brand of newsprint. The art supply store had been out of her usual brand, and on the advice of the clerk she chose this one. She wouldn't even tell me what brand it was, for fear I would tell you and you would tell your friends. Then the whole world would be full of these little stickmen, running around, asking annoying questions.

Whatever the reason behind it, this second figure came to life as well. The newly-drawn eyes watched as the rest of the body was drawn. When the pencil was finally lifted off the paper, the figure walked up and down the length of the sheet, exploring its new home.

"Hooray! You did it!" shouted Sketch, and he waved at the second figure. The other, still trapped in the two dimensions of the page, waved back as best as it could.

The Painter was incredulous, and a little scared. She dashed a line on the paper and waited for it to move, but it didn't. Yet when she drew a third stickman, it came to life just like the other two.

Two sheets of paper and a dozen stickmen later, she understood. If she drew two dots and told herself as she drew them they were only two dots, then they were only two dots. But if she drew them thinking they were eyes, they became eyes. If she drew a big circle around the dots and a slash mark below it, they remained mere marks on the paper—but if she drew them intending to be a head and mouth they became a living head and mouth.

It worked with other things, too. If she drew a line it was just a line—unless she intended it to be something else as she drew it. One line became a snake, a smooth undulation writhing and coiling around the paper. Another became a surface for a stickman to walk upon: when he reached the end, he fell off to the bottom of the paper. Another line became a wall the stickman could not cross. Yet another line became a fence to climb over. A fifth line was the most wonderful of all: it became a doorway to another dimension. The stickman on that page walked behind it and was never seen again.

The Painter tried to explain her findings to Sketch, but he was too excited by all the extra company to listen. Eventually the Painter gave up and handed back the charcoal pencil. She was tired of drawing stickmen. She wanted to paint.

Sketch set out with new inspiration. And you know what? His stickmen came to life as well! Granted, most of his early ones shambled around on wobbly, rickety legs, and some had deformed heads or bent spines. But they were alive!

Several hours later, when he ran out of paper, Sketch arranged all his stickmen on the grass around him. There he tried to teach them, as the Painter had taught him, all about this new world. He spoke learnedly about exoskeletons and kitchen tables and drawing and visions and buttered toast and all other aspects of Great Art. Since he didn't quite understand it himself it came out somewhat muddled, as you can imagine.

The other stickmen dared not question what Sketch was saying. Having no other experience, they believed Sketch knew what he was talking about. They sat quietly and tried to understand, but it made no sense. Plus, they were distracted by a whole world of exciting new things: a passing butterfly, the clouds building in the sky, an ant toiling across the plastic.

The Painter, working on her canvas, didn't know what was going on behind her back. She could hear Sketch talking, but it was a faint scratchy sound and she didn't pay too much attention to it. She was busy painting, but to tell the truth she was more and more preoccupied with the feeling that she getting sick to her stomach.

Maybe it was her breakfast. She had eaten too quickly in her haste to get outside and paint. Or maybe it was the sun now beating down on her, making the white canvas glare. Or maybe it was all the excitement of the past two days. Whatever the reason, she felt awful queasy. It wasn't too bad, yet, so she kept on painting, eager to get as much done as she could.

The legion of stickmen watched in awe as she worked, putting a dab of dark blue here, a smear of light blue there.

"Why is she doing that?" one of the figures asked.

"Be quiet!" Sketch hissed. "Haven't you been listening at all? What have I just been telling you about *vision*? What did I tell you about *technique*? Practice, practice, practice! The Moaning Lisa wasn't mustached in a day, you know!"

This, of course, did not answer the question at all, but luckily for Sketch the stickman didn't want to ask another question and look even more foolish.

"What's she doing now?" another figure asked. The Painter was washing her brush out in the jar of thinner, turning the liquid a bluish color. Sketch was as mystified as the rest.

"Technique," he whispered. "Impressionist art deco. Form and composition. Paper towels and liquid cleanser. Picasso's blue period. Picasso is a painter, you know," he added, for the benefit of those who had never heard of Picasso. "Just like our Painter, only entirely different."

Which again was not an answer, but just a smokescreen of confident words to hide his ignorance. But consider poor Sketch, so recently created, trying desperately to comprehend all the things the Painter had thrown at him. He understood while the Painter was talking, for they were all simple ideas burdened with long names. But now the names were getting all mixed up, and the ideas were tangling together into confusing knots.

He couldn't let on to the other stickmen. They all looked like him and he wanted to stand out. He wanted to prove he was different. He wanted to be seen not just as another stickman, but as an artist, a teacher, just like his beloved Painter.

The Painter shook her brush out over the grass and returned to the canvas. She opened a second can of paint. The stickmen craned their necks to see inside.

In went the brush, glistening brown. The paint was stirred.

Out came the brush—now a bright yellow!

If you could imagine a million daffodils and a million buttercups and a million dandelions in one small can (with an odd lemon or two thrown in for good measure) you could imagine just how yellow this yellow paint was. All of the stickmen gasped "ooooohhhhh!" when they saw it. But the color was secondary to what the Painter did with it. When the yellow mixed with the blue, it produced a wonderful living green.

With short deft strokes, a smear of blue turned into a field of wavy green grass, dotted here and there with yellow grass stems and flowers. The yellow also became the sun, giving warm highlights to everything below in the painting, even piercing some of the dark clouds in the background with golden beams.

The Painter stood back to admire the effect. Beads of sweat were running down her forehead, getting into her eyes. It was beastly hot. The sun was high in the sky, beating viciously down, reflecting off the canvas with an angry glare. And that woozy, sick feeling of hers hadn't gone away. If anything, it was worse.

The Painter glanced behind her. For a minute she forgot her sickness, for a whole sea of eyes were looking back. They belonged to countless stick figures, sitting, standing and squatting on their individual sheets of paper. At their head stood Sketch, his face alight with tentative pride. Most of the stickmen were his own creations. He hoped the Painter would recognize and appreciate all his hard work. He half expected her to hand him the paintbrush right there.

The sight of all those stickmen made the Painter feel even sicker. She was too woozy to care as much as she should have.

"Been busy, I see," she muttered.

"Painter, we have been watching and admiring your work," Sketch said. (He spoke more haughtily now that he had an audience.) "We all want to be artists, like you. I've been teaching them the basics, as you have taught me. Problem is, there's only one charcoal pencil, and I've worn down the point. It does not write anymore. I also need more paper. Can you please give us more supplies?"

"I don't mean to disappoint you, Sketch, but I think I'm going to quit for the day," the Painter replied. "I'm not feeling very well, I'm afraid."

Murmurs of concern spread throughout the crowd of stickmen.

"Don't worry, Painter!" Sketch said. This was his big chance. "I can take over the painting while you rest. I don't need any sleep, you know."

"No, that's okay," the Painter said. "There's a storm coming up. I don't want you or the painting to get wet. Water would ruin you both. Besides, I think you should work on your drawing skills a bit more. Tell you what: I'll take you and your friends back to the house. I'll sharpen your pencil so you can practice drawing some more. But I'm all out of paper. You'll have to make do with the backs of these papers here."

She started gathering the pages of stickmen. They

grew into quite a pile.

Sketch was disappointed again. It seemed no matter how hard he tried, the Painter was not impressed. He wanted her to admire his hard work and reward him—if not with his own paintbrush, at least with heaps of glowing praise.

The Painter, however, never seemed to take the hint. She had no inkling of the turmoil in the stickman's heart. If she did, she would have tried harder to ease his fears, for underneath the gruff exterior she was a kind woman. But she was also a professional. If Sketch really wanted to learn about art he had to learn *properly*.

She noticed a marked improvement as she picked up each sheet of stickmen. The first figures were wobbly and unsure, missing arms, legs and eyes, walking aimlessly in dizzy circles. As Sketch practiced, though, his pencil strokes became firmer, his hand steadier and surer. There was little difference between Sketch's last drawings and her own stickmen.

The Painter pointed this out, but Sketch was too moody to appreciate the compliment. The Painter wasn't feeling well enough to push the matter. She capped the paint, cleaned her brush, and placed everything on the ground near the canvas. She threw the plastic over everything to guard it from the coming rain. She was careful to keep the plastic away from the wet canvas. She then picked up Sketch in one hand and the stack of papers in the other and headed toward the house. Feeling sicker with each step, she dumped everything onto the kitchen table.

"I'm going to bed," she groaned.

"What about my pencil?" Sketch shrieked.

"What about it?"

"It's too dull! I told you I can't draw with it anymore!"

The Painter fumbled in drawer after drawer, searching for a pencil sharpener. All she found was her good stencil-cutter. She whittled the pencil back into a point and slapped it down on the table.

"There, it's sharp now," she snapped. Sketch looked hurt.

"You don't have to be so grumpy about it," he said.

The Painter twiddled the metal knife in her hand. It would be so easy to cut that stickman into little bits with it. Other artists have destroyed greater works of art, she thought. One stickman would not be missed.

Slowly, the feeling of anger passed. She felt tired and guilty. She placed the knife slowly on the table.

"I'm sorry," she admitted, hanging her head. "I didn't mean to snap at you. I'm just not feeling well."

"What's wrong?" Sketch asked, concerned.

"Oh, nothing," the Painter shrugged. "I think I just got too much sun this morning. I think I'll take a nap. I'll be down later. We can talk some more, then. In the meantime—" She picked up the charcoal pencil and handed it to Sketch—"Practice your drawing. You're getting better. Maybe tomorrow I'll find a small canvas for you to paint on."

Sketch stood erect, his eyes widening with pride.

"Yes, ma'am! I'll get to work right away!" He moved toward the pile of papers, then stopped and looked back at the Painter. "I hope you feel better," he said.

"Thank you, Sketch." The Painter managed a half-hearted smile. She was feeling dizzier by the second. "I hope so, too."

Chapter 7

Sketch turned to his work with a joyous shudder. Painting! Him! Sketch! The world was a beautiful place! He looked down at the pile of paper at his feet, searching for a blank spot to draw on. One of the stickmen eyed him from the top page.

"Painting tomorrow, huh?" the stickman said. "Boy, I bet you're excited."

Sketch shrugged, trying to look cool, but he was glowing.

"Yes, that's what she said," he said. "See? If you work hard and keep your vision, you will succeed."

"Then why did the Painter quit just now?" the figure asked. "She said she was sick. Perhaps she's lost her vision?"

"Of course not!" Sketch scoffed. "Our Painter has vision. She gave some to me, so that proves she has it."

"Maybe she gave you too much," the other stickman said. "Perhaps she gave you all the vision she has, and now she can't paint anymore. Maybe she's going to be erased."

Sketch was horrified. The Painter couldn't leave him! He would have to teach all these stickmen about art all by himself! He wasn't ready for such responsibility! He hadn't even touched a paintbrush! But the stickman's suggestion set his imagination afire with all sorts of dreadful ideas. He did his best to shake them out of his mind. He dared not scare the others by panicking himself.

"When she gets erased—I mean, *if* she ever gets erased—I will take over," he said bravely.

"You?" the figure on the paper laughed. "What do you know about things? You've never even painted."

"She said I could start tomorrow."

"But what if she's erased tonight?" the stickman insisted. "What about now?"

"What do you know about it?" Sketch shouted. "Do you think you know more than me? Remember, *I* created *you!*"

"You did not!" the figure on the paper shouted back. "I was made by the Painter herself! I was the first stickman in this whole stack! I watched her make many others before she ever gave you the pencil! I'm just as good as you are!"

"Then why are you still on that page?" Sketch countered hotly. "I have three dimensions, not two. If you're just as good as me, let's see you get off that paper and walk around! Ha! Can't do that, can you, Flattie?"

Flattie's eyes narrowed with anger.

"I suppose you got that way all by yourself?" he sneered. "I'd like to see that!" Sketch had no reply. Flattie pressed his advantage. "Your precious three dimensions only proves you can't replace the Painter," he added. "You don't have the power to release me from the paper. Only the Painter can do that."

Sketch was silent. Flattie had him there. Three-dimensional beings should have three-dimensional ideas, but right now his mind was as flat and blank as an empty piece of paper. Searching for a way to prove his superiority, his eyes rested on the stencil cutter.

"I *can* release you from the paper!" he shouted dramatically, pulling Flattie's page off the stack and standing over him. "You'll have no exoskeleton like mine, but if you'll stand still for a few minutes I'll bring you out here with me."

Flattie didn't believe him at first. When he saw Sketch pick up the stencil cutter he understood, and he was afraid. He knew every inch of his safe, secure, comfortable paper. He was well acquainted with the other stickmen who shared the space with him. What horrible things lurked beyond?

It was too late to back out now. It would never do to show he was scared. Luckily, Sketch's practice with the pencil paid off. He had little difficulty cutting out the figure on the paper—so little, in fact, that he started on the next one, and the next.

After several hours, all of the stickmen—minus an occasional finger or toe—were free of the paper. They could not stand erect, but they could crawl about easily enough on their hands and knees.

The Painter had left the back door open. Outside the trees hissed and shivered, and a humid, twilight draft poured in through the screen. Paper stickmen wafted across the kitchen like so many dead leaves. Soon they were exploring the cabinets and pans and sinks and linoleum and other fascinating objects. A few even slipped under the crack of the screen door, out into the great wide world.

Flattie crawled up to Sketch.

"I'm sorry," he said. "I didn't mean what I said. I didn't think you could do it."

"That's okay, Flattie," Sketch shrugged. To be honest, cutting out the stickmen was so easy he felt a bit disillusioned. He thought it would be some sort of wonderful magic, but anyone with the proper tools could do it. "It was nothing."

"Nothing!" Flattie turned to the others. "He says releasing us is nothing! What else can you do? Can we help? Tell us!"

The stickmen cheered. Sketch was pleased, but nervous. He wondered if he was doing the right thing. He hoped this turn of events wouldn't get the Painter angry. He didn't want to endanger his chances of painting tomorrow.

"Please, guys..." he said, looking at the ground.

"Hey! Over here!"

A stickman crawled back through the crack under the screen door. He was dirt-smeared and wrinkled, but too excited to care.

"The painting!" he shouted. "The Great Painting! It's out there! I saw it!"

The throng buzzed. Several stickmen jumped off the table and countertops to see for themselves. They pushed and clambered for the chance to crawl under the door. As a result, no one could get out.

"Listen, stickmen!" Flattie shouted, standing next to Sketch, supporting himself by leaning against him. "Our beloved Painter is sick! She may be erased at any moment! Her work stands out there undone! She needs our help!"

"How?" someone asked.

"Her successor will show us!" Flattie replied, indicating Sketch. "He will teach us how to paint! We will finish the Great Painting ourselves!"

"Er, now, wait a minute—" Sketch began. The cheers drowned him out. Flattie and a dozen other stickmen pushed him off the table into the waiting arms below. With him protesting all the way, they hustled him out of the kitchen, pushed him through the crack under the door, and out into the world.

Chapter 8

Where was the Painter during all this? In her bed, sound asleep. A raging fever turned her dreams into delirium. She had one of those awful twenty-four hour bugs that hits you like a bulldozer.

She was dreaming the most horrible nightmares, too. The world was full of stick people. They knew nothing of art, and they were too impatient, too intolerant and too two-dimensional to learn. They smiled charcoal pencil smiles like happy-face buttons. Their paper heads were filled with ideas, seemingly substantial but lacking any real depth. As she dreamed, they multiplied until they covered the earth. They swarmed like locusts, leaving a blackish-gray dust over everything they touched.

Let's leave the Painter to her misery and get back to the real stickmen. In the deepening twilight the swarm looked like a long, white snake crawling over the lawn. Hundreds of paper stickmen pushed their way through the grass like jungle explorers. Their sights were set on a huge white, blue, yellow and green monolith that loomed before them. The colored shapes swirled like a dream under the rattling, wavy plastic.

Sketch was experiencing a nightmare of his own, far worse than any other because it was really happening. He knew his chances of painting tomorrow grew dimmer with each step away from the house.

The closer he got to the canvas, however, the more the beauty of the painting entranced him. He forgot about tomorrow and concentrated on today. It was so near, so beautiful, so colorful. He could add to that beauty and color. He just *knew* it. The magic of possibility filled him. All thoughts of the Painter were swept away as the clear plastic was dragged off, right on top of everyone.

Being the strongest, Sketch was the first out from under. He helped draw the plastic away from the others. The painting got a little smudged. The plastic sheet was covered with smears of paint. Sketch touched one. It came off on his hand, a sticky blue goo. He paddled in a yellow spot with his other hand, then slapped his hands together and rubbed it all into green.

His gaze drew from his hands to that last unopened can of paint. Color was such a wonderful thing! What could that last mystery color possibly be like?

"That one!" he commanded. "We must open that can first!"

It was much harder than the Painter made it look. Eventually the stickmen managed to hook the tip of the brush handle under the metal lip and pry the lid off the can. Sketch climbed up onto the nearby can of blue paint and peered inside.

The light was failing rapidly now. There was barely enough to see. The pool of liquid in the can was by far the most exciting color the stickman had ever seen: a deep, bloody red. The blue and yellow spoke of airy, natural things, of sky and light and grass. The red was something else again. It brooded with anger; it pulsed with life. Sketch was taken aback. The red paint glared; a watchdog left by the Painter to protect her work. It growled at Sketch, ready to attack.

As Sketch stepped back, the stickmen put the brush in his hands. Its sturdy weight gave him courage. He had a weapon. He stabbed at the paint as it lurked in the can. His brush dripped bright red drops on the grass below. He hoisted the brush clear of the can, swung it over and slapped it against the canvas.

It was much heavier and harder to control than he imagined. The brush was wider than the pencil point, more flexible and changeable. But oh, the color it made! Back and forth, back and forth he swished the brush, until he ran out of paint and a big red smear stood out on the painting. He dipped his brush and painted again. He forgot all the others around him, mindful only of the joy of color.

The other stickmen were awed at first. The sight of the red paint on the canvas struck them with a fever of desire. Individually they were too weak to hold a brush, but they dipped their hands into the paint and smeared it on the canvas that way. The paint made their paper hands stick to the canvas. They had to peel themselves away.

That gave Flattie an idea. He coated his hands and knees with paint and crawled right up the side of the painting like a fly. The paint stuck him to the surface and left a red trail in his wake. Others were quick to copy him. Before long many stickmen had crawled to the top of the canvas. They looked around and laughed and threw handfuls of paint onto their friends below.

They eventually tired of red and opened the other two cans. The activity and excitement increased with each color added. There were paint-splattered stickmen everywhere. It was a mob! They chattered nonstop as they splashed paint around. The original painting slowly disappeared under the layers of splattered paint.

A low rumble caused everyone to look up. Above the towering canvas the sky had grown quite dark. The air was stuffy and humid. Sketch felt a pang of conscience, a vaguely remembered warning. Why didn't the Painter leave him outside with the painting? Something about a storm, whatever that was—and getting wet.

Filling with fear and guilt, he looked up at the canvas with new eyes. The picture had lost its appeal. Once so beautiful, it was now a muddy travesty. The others were still working, slashing paint on with wild strokes, crawling all over the sticky, messy cloth. All the beautiful colors had blended together into an unattractive mud brown. Scars of brilliant red showed through as though the canvas was bleeding.

Was it? He saw one tiny section of color swell and trickle down the surface—and then another, and another. What was happening?

Just then a large drop of water hit him on his cardboard back, a glancing blow. Another hit him on the arm, wet and dangerous. As he jumped back in alarm, the paper bubbled and wrinkled and drew away from the cardboard. The dark charcoal line of his arm weeped gray tears. A shooting pain spread up his arm, up his neck, into his head. So he *could* feel pain, he thought to himself. Then he panicked.

"The storm!" he screamed. "The storm!"

His words were lost in a rumble of thunder. The other stickmen ignored him. He looked desperately over at the house. It was only a few yards away, but a fantastically long distance to him. He could never make it in time. The rain was coming down harder. His arm was already feeling soft and flabby. With his remaining strength he jumped off the paint can.

"The storm!" he repeated.

It was no use. He stumbled under the plastic, leaving the others to their fate.

Chapter 9

The Painter awoke, from force of habit, at dawn. Although still feverish and weak, the worst part seemed to be over. The memory of her sickness stayed in the back of her mind like a bad dream. She felt groggy and confused. She was not sure how long she was sick. She wasn't sure what was real and what wasn't anymore.

She got out of bed, put on her ratty old bathrobe, splashed some water on her face, and went downstairs. It looked like it rained the night before. She worried about her canvas. She decided to check on it before breakfast, bare feet and all.

The kitchen, strangely enough, was littered with paper. It looked like an entire pad of newsprint had been chopped into confetti and blown all over the room. The smooth wooden surface of her good table was covered with scratches. Her stencil cutter was stuck, point down, into the linoleum below. Clearly it had rolled off the table. The Painter pulled the knife out of the floor and examined the ruined blade. A dreadful, funny feeling washed over her sick body.

The door was open. She couldn't remember if she had closed it before she went to bed. Perhaps some vandals snuck in while she was asleep and made this mess? She was unpopular in the neighborhood, she knew, but not enough for this.

Funny, she thought. Those nightmares had seemed so real. She opened the screen door and walked out onto the porch.

The painting was ruined. The wind had torn the plastic off the canvas, exposing it to the driving rain. It was a sodden mess of gray-brown smudge. Hopeless.

The storm had blown a great deal of trash into her yard. The grass was littered with bits of paper. More paper was plastered to the canvas, matted like leaves in a gutter. Her mouth dry, the Painter picked one up off the ground nearby. It was smeared with paint and soggy with rain. It also bore a few streaks of gray—a faint outline of a charcoal stickman.

Before her sick mind could fully comprehend what was happening, the plastic moved. Something was alive underneath. What was it? A mouse? A rabbit?

No! It was Sketch. Still mostly dry, his paper only curling slightly away from his cardboard backing, he staggered to his feet. One arm had separated from the cardboard and dangled from his body, half-ripped and useless. His head hung meekly as he awaited a response from the speechless Painter.

jkflaiuh blu fkb kvjl jnk
vblh j b,k ;JA fhljkh ;I
t.b;lUH;SJBlKNlkxuhPOI UH ISJBO;IZ LJPOF
J KNKSU GPD ABCDEFGHIJKLMNOPQRSTUVWXYZ
ABCDEFGHIJKLMNOPQRSTUVWXYZ
    HOUSEPAINTSKETCHSKETCH
SKETCHSTICKDRAWINGBRUSHCANVAS PAINTING
PENCIL HELLO HOW ARE YOU I AM FINE I AM
PRACTICING RIGHTING SO I WILL BE A BETTER
WRITER THAN HER OF COURSE SHE HAS MORE
PRACTICE CUZ SHE HOGS THE COMPUTER ALL
THE TIME AND DOESN'T LET ME WRITE AS OFFEN
AS I LIKE. SHE PLAYS TOO MANY COMPUTER
GAMES! SHE TELLS PEOPLE SHE'S WRITING
BUT THEN SHE GOES AND PLAYS GAMES ON THE
COMPUTER FOR HOURS. THIS IS TOO EASY I
DON'T SEE WHY SHE SAYS IT'S SO MUCH WORK.
IT'S NOT WORKING, IT'S JUST HOPPING UP
AND DOWN ON THE KEYS.

Chapter 10

"You're probably going to think I'm crazy."

One look at her wild eyes and unkempt hair and I didn't *think*. I *knew*. She looked like she had just dragged herself out of bed after a long illness. She was barefoot, and still in her bathrobe. Nobody in their right mind leaves the house looking like that, let alone hike half a mile down a dirt road to the neighbor's house.

"May I come in?" she asked.

I was still standing there, mouth open like a hooked fish, blocking her path. I was too shocked to answer politely. I grunted something and ushered her inside.

"I hope I'm not disturbing you," she said.

"Oh, no. Not at all," I lied. "I was just writing. Nothing important. Just...stuff."

"I can come back."

"No, no, it's quite all right. I was just about to take a break and make myself a sandwich. Can I get you something? Want some breakfast?"

She blanched. "No, thank you."

She spoke tersely, hardly waiting for me to finish. I thought she might be weirded out because I was having a sandwich for breakfast. I've always eaten weird things at weird times. Sometimes I have spaghetti or pizza for breakfast. Sometimes I have pancakes or cold cereal for dinner. Sometimes I just have a big slab of cake and leave it at that. As I prepared my sandwich she sat at the kitchen table and stared at the wall. She didn't want to look at the food.

"You don't look too well," I said. "Have you been sick?"

"A bit,"" she nodded. "The worst of it's over, I think. Upset stomach."

I tossed my sandwich onto the table and poured myself a glass of milk. I hated eating in front of her. I felt rude, and to be honest having a really sick person in my house made me feel kind of sick, myself. But I was starving.

"So, what's new in the world of art?" I asked, slightly muffled by bread.

She gave me such a look it was all I could do to swallow. It was almost as if she *knew*. But no—that was silly. She couldn't possibly know.

"Nothing's new," she said, her eyes boring into mine. "What's new with you?"

"Nothing."

There was an uncomfortable pause that felt like a minor eternity.

"Are you working on anything?" I finally asked.

"Just a painting," she said. "It's not going too well, though. How about you?"

"Nothing much. Just a story. It's not going very well, either."

"Magazine article?"

"No. Fiction this time. Just a little something I've been working on. Can you please excuse me for a second?"

Visitors to other people's homes usually don't notice strange noises, but a quiet, erratic tapping had started from my office and it was driving me crazy. I stuck my head out of the kitchen.

"Hey! Cut it out in there!" I shouted. The noise stopped.

"It's my cat," I explained as I came back to the table. "She's fascinated by the computer. She likes to bat at the keys with her paws when I'm not there."

"I have that same problem," the Painter smiled.

I looked at her funny.

"You don't have a cat," I said. "Do you?"

She squirmed in her chair. I sat back down, but my sandwich was forgotten. The Painter grabbed my hand. I tried not to think that she was probably still swarming with upset stomach germs.

"Look, I have to tell you something. You have to promise not to breathe a word of this to anyone. Do you understand? *No one.*"

There was no escaping those relentless eyes. My mouth was too dry to speak. All I could do was nod my head. The noise in the other room resumed: a gentle tap-tap, tap-tap. It echoed through the entire house.

"Could you please excuse me again?" I forced a twisted embarrassed smile and backed toward the door.

"I SAID *NO!*" I bellowed down the hallway. "BAD CAT! DO YOU HEAR ME? *BAD CAT!*"

Still smiling, I sat back down at the table.

"How many cats do you have?" the Painter asked.

"Just the one," I said. "One too many, sometimes."

"Then who's that?" She was pointing behind me. My chair squeaked on the floor as I turned to look. Nothing out of the ordinary. Just my cat, eating food out of her dish. Tap-tap, the noise came back, louder this time. Tap-tap, tap-tap-tap.

I looked at the Painter, trying not to look guilty. She looked at me, realization dawning over her face.

"Sketch!" she gasped.

We both raced for the hallway. She's pretty spry for her age. She reached the door to my office well ahead of me and flung it open. There stood Sketch on the keyboard, hopping up and down on the keys.

"Hey! Cut that out!" I shouted, dashing into the room. "I told you not to touch that!"

Sketch looked up from his work.

"There's a couple of parts I don't like," he said. "I just thought I'd change them myself. I figured you wouldn't mind."

"Of course I mind!" I shrieked. "Its *my* story, not yours! Don't touch it, okay? Just leave it alone!"

"No, it's *my* story," Sketch insisted. "It's all about *me*. You're in it, of course. So's the Painter. But it's *mine*."

"It was *you*." The Painter stared at me. "You put me in a story, didn't you? All this time I thought I was going nuts. It was *you* all along."

"Look, I'm sorry," I said. "It's just a story, you know? It's not supposed to *really* happen."

"Well, it *did* happen," she frowned. "And now you've got to fix it. It's bad enough you made me sick as a dog. You have me lying in bed delirious with the flu while you're eating sandwiches and playing computer games. It's not fair!"

"I know!" Sketch agreed, excited. "That's one of the parts I was trying to change! I didn't think it was very nice, making you so sick."

"You be quiet!" I turned on Sketch. I was really angry, now. "And leave my story alone! I won't have you ruining it the way you ruined her painting!"

One look at Sketch's face stopped me cold. Ever say something mean, and then really wish you could take it back the instant you said it? The look on his face will haunt me the rest of my life.

"I'm sorry, Sketch," I mumbled. "I didn't mean that. I just want you to ask next time before you mess with my stuff."

"I'm only trying to help," he sniffled.

"Why don't you come home with me and practice your brushwork?" the Painter suggested. (You see? She really is a nice person. Much nicer than I am.)

"But what about—you know," I didn't want to say it out loud. "The rain—paint—thunder—you know... the painting?"

Sketch looked guilty. The Painter answered for him.

"Destroyed," she nodded. "But these things happen. I can't count the number of canvases I ruined when I first tried to paint. He'll never learn if he never makes mistakes."

"I don't think I want to be a painter," Sketch said. "I want to be a writer."

"You can't be a writer!" I insisted. "You don't know the first thing about it."

"You could teach him," the Painter said. "You made me teach him about painting. Why can't you teach him about writing?"

"Why? Because.... because I—" I fumbled for words and then flopped down in my office chair. Sketch climbed down off the keyboard and sat on the edge of my desk, his legs swinging into space. He waited for me to say something.

"You know, Sketch," I said. "If you go back with the Painter I can fix it so everything goes right. The canvas won't be ruined. You'll learn how to paint. You'll make a million dollars. You can live happily ever after."

"You could," Sketch agreed. "But it wouldn't be very believable."

"He's got that right!" the Painter laughed. She leaned against the wall and folded her arms across her chest. "And you say he's not a writer? He's a natural!"

"I don't think you two are very good judges of believability," I snorted. "I don't know which is more unbelievable, talking to a piece of paper, or having the paper talk back to you."

"You thought it was okay when it was happening to the Painter," Sketch said.

I sighed, blowing out my cheeks and staring at the ceiling. Sketch watched me, nervously.

"Tell you what," he suggested. "Let me finish this story for you. If it's no good, I'll find something else to do, and I won't bother you again. I promise."

I looked at him for a good long while. He wasn't such a bad character. A little flat, perhaps. But we can't *all* be exciting, now, can we? And when you get right down to it, everyday life is pretty dull. It's nice and all, but it's not the amusement park ride people expect it to be. Real joy is found in a quiet daily contentment, flopped on the couch, perhaps, with a cat in your lap or a dog at your feet or a loved one lounging nearby. Not always saying anything or writing anything or painting anything, but just sitting quietly, your family and friends puttering around you, living their lives while you live yours. Messing up, making mistakes, starting over again.

But I couldn't let go. The story was mine, not his. And I didn't want it turned into another muddy, sticky mess.

"Why should I let *you* write my ending?" I grumbled.

Sketch looked me full in the face, not flinching.

"Because you're not a very good writer," he said. "You're just going to mess it up."

The Painter burst out laughing again. I waved my hand in her direction to shut her up, never taking my eyes off the stickman.

"What do you mean by that?" I said.

"You use too many different words," Sketch explained. "You're always talking about stuff. Art. Life. Love. Joy. Learning. You write like they're all different things, but they're not. They're all the same. You can't tell where one stops and the other begins. It's all one thing. So using all those different words to talk about it just confuses people."

He fell silent. I was silent. The Painter was silent. That's how the cat found us. She came into the room, meowed her rusty squeak of a meow, and rubbed against my leg. Then she jumped into my lap and curled up, purring, to go to sleep. I pet her without even thinking about it, scratching her behind the ears the way cats like to be scratched, feeling her tiny warm throat vibrate under my fingers.

You know, beautiful, famous art is available in any museum or gallery. It doesn't take much of an effort to see it. Go see it, I say, and see if you can get some great famous work of art to talk to you. I've gone many times, with the Painter, with a friend, or by myself. It's sort of fun, seeing a famous painting. It's a little like meeting a famous person. Problem is, unlike a human celebrity, famous art doesn't shut up and leave you alone when you excuse yourself. It doesn't take the hint. It keeps following you and talking to you. There's no escaping it.

And you don't need to go to a museum, if you don't feel like it. A child's drawing on the refrigerator has said as much to me as any Monet or Renoir. Maybe it can't use big giant words or big giant ideas, but it *does* have something to say. So does something as simple as a stickman. Exactly what, I don't know. I guess we'll just have to wait and find out.

I stood up and deposited the cat alone on the chair. Leaving the office, I walked down the hall to the front door and opened it.

"Sketch, the world is spread out before you," I announced. "The possibilities are endless. I hope you'll treat others with more kindness than I've shown you. Beyond that, you're on your own."

Sketch brightened.

"I will! And I'll be brave and famous and good and rich and talented! Can I use your computer? I want to start right away!"

"No, I need it," I said. "But you can use this...."

I hunted through my desk drawer and handed him a pencil. He smiled and cradled it in his arms, like an old friend. Then he was gone, scampered off, eager to begin his new life.

How does this story turn out? I don't know; he's still writing it. Besides, what do I know? I am but a mere fiction, a literary device. I am a figment in a stickman's mind, a bit player on a stage he has set for himself. There's a Painter in here too, somewhere, along with many other people he has met, or that he someday hopes to meet.

We are real people to Sketch, but some people don't see us. All they see are scratches of pigment on a piece of paper. They'll laugh at us if our noses look funny, but otherwise they ignore us. It's just as well. We're just stickmen to them, all the same, passing them anonymously on the street. They'll laugh and tell you anyone can draw a stickman. Yep, anyone can. But we're more than that, just as a stickman is more than a stickman. We are all intertwined works of art: too many for Sketch to count, to write about, or to paint in one lifetime.

Once in a while Sketch stops by for a visit. The Painter tells me she sees him too, on occasion. He never stays for long. Just a brief visit, and then he's gone again, living his own life.

We miss him and think of him often, the Painter and I. If you should happen to see him, say hi for us. Then drop me a line and tell me what he's up to. I'd like to hear how he's doing.

The End